THE MICE

at Amsterdam Centraal Station

PAGE PUBLISHING, INC.
Conneaut Lake, PA

First originally published by Page Publishing 2021

ISBN 978-1-6624-2964-4 (pbk)
ISBN 978-1-6624-2965-1 (digital)

Printed in the United States of America

THE MICE

at Amsterdam Centraal Station

Mark Kash

As usual, Papa came home from work at 5:30 p.m. "Guess what I brought you," he said as he put away his hat and coat.

"I'm sure I don't know," Mama called back from the kitchen as she was making supper for Papa and the rest of the family.

Papa had brought home a round disc with shiny gold trim and a silver center. "A mirror," he replied to Mama as he made his way into the kitchen. "One of the passengers dropped it onto the tracks during my shift," he said. "I barely had enough time to remove it before the 1:20 p.m. train pulled into the station."

Papa worked as a safety engineer for the Amsterdam City Railway. It was his job to inspect the tracks and remove debris that could harm the trains. Papa worked at the Amsterdam Centraal Station on track 11A. The family lived in a four-room apartment just two floors below the tracks.

"Just put it in the hallway, and I will get Clovis to help me hang it up tomorrow," Mama said as she finished putting the supper in the oven.

Clovis was the oldest of the two mice children. He had recently finished school and was expected to follow in his father's footsteps becoming a safety engineer for the Amsterdam Railway. However, Clovis had dreams of his own. Clovis spent all his free time down at Schiphol Airport, watching the flying trains, as he called them, flying passengers in and out of the city. "One day, I am going to be a great adventurer," Clovis would always say. Zuri, the mice's youngest son, was just old enough to start school and was extremely excitable. Zuri always wants to be in the middle of the action—whatever it is.

"Wash up for supper and tell Grandpa to wake up and do the same," Mama said. "Supper will be ready any minute now."

Papa went to the living room and gently shook Grandpa, who was napping on the couch. Grandpa let out a couple of grunts, grabbed the blanket, and began to roll over. The blanket, however, was tucked up underneath Grandpa from hours of napping, and this time, it didn't give. Holding firm, the tight blanket pulled back against Grandpa, rolling him back over and right onto the floor. With a firm thud, Grandpa woke up on the floor to the sound of muffled chuckling from Papa standing over him. "Have a good nap?" Papa asked as best he could between laughs.

3

"Darned old tail," Grandpa said with a huff. "That'd never happen if I still had my tail." This is what Grandpa always said when he fell off the couch while napping, which he did quite often. Grandpa had retired from the Amsterdam Railway several years back after losing his tail in a railway accident. He lost his tail in the conductor strike of '04. Inexperienced substitute conductors had failed to see the line had switched rails and were speeding toward the station too fast. A train was about to crash into another train still in the station before Grandpa leapt across the track and threw the switch. Grandpa saved the train and became a hero, but at a cost. And in case you forgot, Grandpa was always happy to remind you how he saved the train but lost his tail.

Grandpa was still muttering about his tail as the family gathered in the kitchen for supper. "Oh, Grandpa," Mama exclaimed, "this tall tale of yours is getting longer than your real tail ever was." Everyone laughed, except for Grandpa, who was sure every bit was true—even the parts he made up.

"So, Clovis," Papa inquired, "when are you going to apply for a job at the railway? I could put in a good word for you."

Clovis didn't answer right away. He knew that his parents wouldn't approve of his dream of going off on the flying trains. Clovis tried to choose his words carefully. "I thought I would take the summer to look around a bit and then decide," Clovis said cautiously. Clovis figured this would give him time to find a ride on the flying trains and start his life as an adventurer.

"What's wrong with working on the railway?" Grandpa interjected excitedly. "We mice have always worked for the railway, seven generations, and not once did we ever have anyone not work for the railway," Grandpa continued. "It's in our blood."

Grandpa was right—sort of. It's true that for seven generations, they have always had a mouse working for the Amsterdam Railway, but it wasn't true that no one had ever *not* worked for the railway.

Grandpa had three brothers who didn't go to work for the Amsterdam Railway. The first, Jake, had moved to Germany and began working for the Berlin Railway at the Zoo Station. The second, Jasper, stayed in Amsterdam but went to work at The Donkey and Scissors, an English pub in Dam Square. The third, Jules, left Europe and went to America, settling down in Napa Valley, California, becoming an importer/exporter of fine cheeses. Grandpa never spoke to his brothers, but he always ate the cheese log he received for Christmas.

"Well, I wouldn't think about it too long," Papa said assertively. "They are hiring right now, and I think they may be changing some of the requirements soon." Papa didn't want to say too much so as not to worry Mama. However, the railway was looking at making some changes—and not for the better as far as Papa was concerned.

Clovis's best friend was a field mouse named Ian. He lived with his family just outside of Amsterdam. Ian's father had a farm where they raised tulip bulbs to sell to tourists who came to the city. Every year, Ian's father would enter his tulip bulbs in a contest to have them grown and shown at the Keukenhof, a large botanical garden that is only open during spring when the tulips are in bloom. The Keukenhof is the premier showcase for tulips with over two million bulbs in bloom. Clovis would often go help Ian tend to the

bulbs on the farm, turning the soil and pulling weeds. He did this because afterward, Ian's mother would bake them cupcakes, which, as Clovis put it, "is what every adventurer should eat."

Clovis and Ian had taken the train out to Schiphol Airport to watch the flying trains, as they often did. They both dreamed of far-off adventure, but Ian asked Clovis a question this time that made it all too real—and close to home. "Does your dad know you don't want to follow in his footsteps?" Ian asked earnestly.

Clovis knew this was a question Ian was asking himself as well. "No, I haven't told them yet," Clovis replied. "I know he will be really disappointed."

Clovis knew Ian didn't want to be a farmer, but his dad would never allow him to go off to see the world. As far as Ian's father was concerned, their farm was the world, and he expected Ian to take over the family business once he got enough experience. Ian didn't mind the work; he just wanted more than a farmer's life, but he couldn't see any way out of it. Clovis started to ask Ian the same question—but glanced over at Ian and could see by his expression that that was something Ian had not talked about with his father either. Clovis looked down at his feet as he kicked a pebble across the ground. "It's all he talks about now that school is over. But I want to see the world, get out on my own…" Clovis's voice trailed off. He knew this would be difficult to get Papa to understand.

Ian looked at him for a moment, then turned away toward the train platform. Ian knew just how Clovis felt because he knew he would be taking over the family business and was going to grow tulip bulbs right there on the farm. "Come on," Ian said to Clovis.

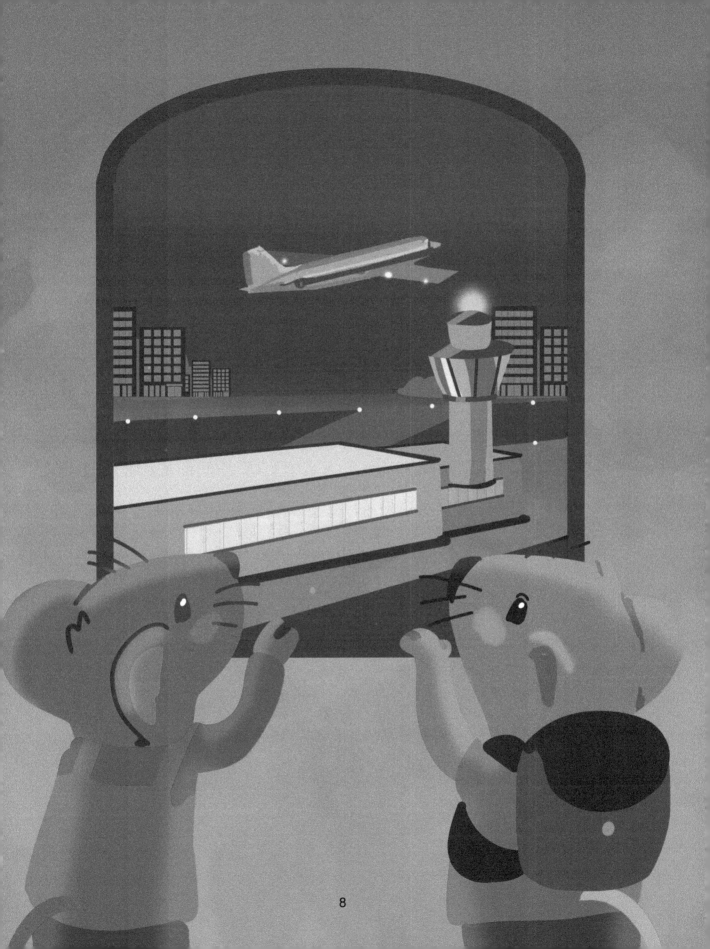

"Let's head to town and go see a movie." Ian pressed Clovis, "We're not deciding the rest of our lives tonight, are we?"

"No, I guess not," Clovis replied. "You're right, let's have some fun. A…a movie sounds great!"

Clovis took one last look at the flying train as it taxied down the runway, then took a skip start as he went to catch up with Ian, who was almost to the platform for the train into town.

"Hey, wait up, Ian," Clovis called out, exasperated. "And this time, don't shut the door and make me wait for the next train."

Ian said nothing, but grinned sheepishly and mischievously as the train rolled into the station.

A few weeks later, the changes at the railroad were announced. The railway had decided to replace their mice safety engineers with cats. They had been testing the cats out on the outer railway lines between stations, and now they were ready to replace the workers in the stations as well. All the mice working the lines went to the union about it, but they were informed that the railway management had conformed to proper procedures, and nothing could be done. All the mice were going to be laid off—including Papa!

The railroad hired a large older cat called Mr. Zips to be in charge of the new cat safety engineers. He had mottled gray fur that swayed like tallgrass in a breeze when he moved. It was ironic that his name was Mr. Zips because he waddled a bit when he walked and wasn't very fast at all.

The cats were indeed faster. They could inspect and cover more of the rail track in less than half the time of the mice. However, the cats weren't as meticulous as the mice were, and so problems occurring on the lines began to increase. Mr. Zips was good at getting his paperwork done, but since he was so slow to get around, he hardly ever went out to check any of the cats' work on the rail lines, and if he did, it was only the rail line that lay adjacent to his office. The cat safety engineers had a bad habit of racing down the tracks in a hurry, barely scanning the rail lines and surrounding area for potential issues that could create problems for the railway.

Also, the cats refused to go out at all if the weather was bad. Top management had made up their minds however, and they were not going to admit they may have made this decision a little too hastily.

Papa looked for work all over the city. He finally found a job as a night watch mouse in the Van Gogh Museum. Van Gogh was a famous Dutch painter in the nineteenth century, and his paintings are worth millions of dollars to collectors. Papa roamed the halls of the exhibits and made sure all the paintings were where they were supposed to be. If something was wrong, Papa would notify the police and the museum curators by pushing the alarm signal. There was an alarm signal button in every hall so Papa could notify the police right away. Also, it would tell them in which precise room the trouble was found. Papa liked the work and enjoyed marveling at all the art pieces—except for one. The painting titled *Wheatfield with Crows*. That painting always reminded him of the time before the peace between the crows and the mice. They would come out of the sky from nowhere and grab friends or family right in front of you, and they would never be seen again. Yes, that painting always sent a chill down Papa's spine, and he took great care to pass that painting as faraway as possible.

Zuri was too small to go out into the city by himself, so Mama would almost always insist on Clovis taking him along whenever he and Ian went out. This meant that they had to keep quiet about their adventure dreams when he was with them—Clovis didn't want Zuri to tell Mama and Papa about his plans. Zuri almost never listened to Clovis and Ian talking anyway; he was too busy taking in all the sights and just happy not being stuck at home.

One afternoon, Clovis really wanted to go watch the flying trains and made plans with Ian to meet at the airport, but Mama caught him as he headed out the door. "Don't forget your little brother," she called out as Clovis grabbed for the handle to pull the door shut behind him.

He thought about pretending he didn't hear her. However, Clovis knew that would be worse when he came home rather than just letting Zuri tag along. "But… Ian and I already have plans," Clovis protested as he stepped back halfway through the doorway.

He had hoped for an, "All right, you can go—this time," from Mama, but instead, he got *the look*. He knew what that look meant, and he was not going to win this argument. "I have cleaning and laundry to do," Mama said sternly, not giving up *the look* until she was sure he got the message. "And I don't want Zuri underfoot."

"Yes, Mama," Clovis replied, exasperated. "Come on, Zuri, I don't want to miss the train."

Zuri gave an exalted, "Yippee, the train!" grabbed his coat, and bounded out the door. Clovis shrugged begrudgingly and sighed loudly as he closed the door behind them. Mama just smiled wryly and went about her housework, knowing Clovis was being overly melodramatic.

Clovis was going to the airport, little brother or not, so he made sure this time Zuri was listening. "You cannot tell Mama and Papa where I am going, you got that?" Clovis said flatly and directly. "This one is a secret."

Zuri, who usually just let Clovis's directions pass without notice, could tell there was something different about this—and it wasn't just the word *secret*. Zuri stopped his skipping about and turned

13

to look Clovis in the eyes. Clovis looked back. "I mean it, Zuri, or I will *never* take you with me again." Clovis emphasized the word *never* and hung on it a little longer to get his point across.

Zuri blinked. He looked at Clovis, all the while turning his head sideways—as if trying figure out a problem. Zuri liked to ask questions, but even as young as he was, he knew from Clovis' tone of voice that this was not one of those times.

"Okay…" Zuri almost whispered his response, "I promise." He held out his hand for Clovis to take. Then he walked beside Clovis, happily thinking he had just grown up some. Alright, he did skip a little.

Ian caught sight of Clovis and Zuri as they exited the train. He hadn't expected Zuri to tag along and gave a quizzical, if not somewhat disappointed, look Clovis' way as they approached. Clovis stopped him before he could even get the words out. "Mama didn't give me a choice…" Clovis replied to Ian's implied question. "This was the only way she would let me go out."

"But, what if he talks?" Ian protested. "Your folks will tell my folks, and then we'll never be able to pl——"

"Quiet," Clovis shot back in a demanding tone under his breath, cutting Ian off mid-sentence. "I already spoke to Zuri and he is not going to say a thing…are you?"

Zuri had been quite content to have taken the train and was looking at the people hustling about on the platform. He heard his name; and turned in time to catch the end of the sentence, and both Clovis and Ian glaring at him. "What?" Zuri replied, not really knowing the question. The looks, however, made it quite clear. "Oh no, I am not going to say anything to anyone, I want to hang out with you more. I won't say anything, I promise."

"Satisfied?" Clovis asked Ian, trying to put the conversation to rest. Ian wasn't entirely convinced, but the situation wasn't going to change itself by arguing the point.

Clovis and Ian headed toward the viewing window so they could get a good look at the flying trains. Zuri had already forgotten the previous conversation as he excitedly ran up ahead to get the best view. Clovis gave Ian a playful push, and Ian shot back a slight grin, then broke out into a full run, hollering back, "Last one there is a rotted tulip."

Clovis and Ian watched the flying trains, making up stories about the people who were traveling on them. Each of them trying to outdo the other with the most ridiculous scenario they could think up. Every once in a while, Zuri would hear part of a story and fall over laughing as if it were the funniest thing he had ever heard—even if he didn't know what they were saying. Soon, however, the sky had grayed and it was time to go home.

"We had better be getting back," Ian said wistfully. "My folks don't like it when I am gone past dark."

"Yeah," Clovis replied. "It's some ways back home, and Mama will be mad we missed supper."

The two friends took one last look at the Flying Train taxiing down the runway and then speeding off into the sky. *Soon*, Clovis thought to himself as he, Zuri, and Ian ambled over to the platform to wait for their train. The station at the airport was nearly empty this time of night, and they were in no hurry to get home.

A couple of weeks passed, and summer was nearing a close. Papa had said no more about the railroad since there were no jobs to be had, but he was insisting that Clovis find some work to help support the family. Clovis knew he was running out of time. It was just a conversation he did not want to face.

Trying to find the courage and words he would need to convince Papa, Clovis went to the one place where he could clear his mind and think—Schiphol Airport. There was a calmness among the chaos of travelers, shuffling to meet their planes or reuniting with loved ones after their trip. *You can't find adventure living at home*, Clovis thought to himself as he settled into his favorite viewing spot.

As Clovis sat watching the flying trains arriving and departing from Schiphol, he knew in his heart that he wanted to be an adventurer. Now he just had to break the news to his family. He had made up his mind and was leaving Amsterdam in the morning, he told himself—he just needed to let them know.

While Clovis was at the airport, a terrible storm had been forming overhead. The skies had darkened and the wind began to howl. The cats, who had replaced the mice as safety engineers, were supposed to check the tracks for problems during bad weather. Instead, they took shelter inside their office to wait out the storm. Mr. Zips did nothing to dissuade the cats from taking shelter, believing the storm would pass uneventfully and the cats could survey the tracks when the rain had subsided. While they waited, a branch from a large tree located alongside the train route had snapped and blew onto the middle of the train tracks. This was going to be a very bad storm.

Clovis turned around from the viewing window and made his way to the train platform for the ride back home. He braced himself against the wind, wishing he had brought a coat. Clovis shook off the rain as he boarded the train that had just pulled into the station. Clovis knew his father, who had been a safety engineer nearly all his life, would be disappointed, but with the cats taking over their jobs, he hoped his father would ultimately understand.

The train drew out of the airport terminal and began to pick up speed as it made its way through the countryside back toward Amsterdam Centraal Station. Clovis sat alone in the train car and watched out the window as the rain began to beat against the glass and trail down in a zigzag motion. He watched silently as the train sped past the pastures and houses that dotted the land between the airport and town. He thought of the far off adventures that awaited him when suddenly there was a crashing noise that came from below the train.

The train, speeding along its route, had run over the large branch that had fallen on the tracks. As the train rolled over the bushy leaves of the branch, it caused the other end of the broken branch to jump up like a teeter-totter and tumble and crash against the underside of the train as it sped down the track. While the branch turned over and over, it kept damaging the train underneath until finally severing a brake line on the train car in which Clovis was riding. The brake line started spilling the brake fluid across the track, which created a loss of pressure that was needed to slow and stop the train. Clovis was tossed out of his seat as the train lurched briefly before the weight and speed of the train forced the branch to be broken and splintered across the tracks as the remaining train cars passed harmlessly overhead. Clovis picked himself up and once again sat back in his seat, all the while wondering what it was that caused the train to behave that way, unaware of the danger ahead.

At first, it wasn't known how badly the branch had damaged the train. Now approaching a passenger platform, Clovis could see that the train was not slowing down in order to stop at this station. Clovis knew that the train always stopped here, and if it was speeding past, something must have gone wrong. Growing up, Clovis spent many hours walking the tracks with Papa, learning how the trains run and the importance of the safety engineers' job. "I wonder if that crash below the train car had anything to do with it," Clovis said to himself as he sat there, now puzzled by what had just happened.

Clovis got up from his seat and made his way to the front of the train car as the train continued to accelerate down the track.

By this time, he knew the train was in trouble and figured that the crashing jolt under the car must be the reason. Clovis opened the door of the train and stepped outside. The storm was surging, and the cold rain stung his fur. He struggled to keep his balance as the wind whipped along the track but finally made his way beneath the train to investigate the cause of the crashing jolt.

It didn't take him long. In the shadowy darkness, Clovis could see the severed brake line dangling wildly from underneath the train car. He could also see the brake fluid draining from the line. As Clovis surveyed the damaged brake line, the train passed the next passenger platform on its way to Amsterdam Centraal Station. He knew that this was the last stop before the train arrived at the Centraal terminal, and he also knew that with the storm, the platforms would be full of commuters and other folks just trying to stay out of the rain. Also, since his train didn't make its scheduled stops along the route, there would be another train still in the terminal when they arrived. Clovis had to act right away.

Clovis climbed his way underneath the train to try and grab one of the dangling brake lines. It was difficult to see because the wind whooshed underneath the train, and the raindrops bounced off the tracks so hard that they hit him in the face.

Quickly and carefully, Clovis felt his way along the plethora of wet and dangerous moving parts. One wrong move, and he would be either thrown from the train or wrapped up in the deadly machinery through which he climbed. At last, he made his way to one of the brake lines. Looking at it, he could tell that the end was damaged. He thought to himself, *If only there is a way to get the pieces to fit?* Then the answer came to him in a flash! If he could repair one side of the line; then he could grab the other line and push the two together.

Clovis had a plan. He began to nibble and chew on the damaged end of the line until it looked like the end of a needle. Now all he had to do was grab the other line and slip the two together. But how? The other line was on the other side of the train car, and they were rapidly approaching the station. Clovis knew he only had one chance. He had come this far—he had to try! Taking a deep breath, Clovis grabbed the brake line in one hand, took a running leap, and swung himself toward the other dangling line. The other line flew wildly as it dangled on its side of the train car. Clovis stretched himself as much as he possibly could and—scooped up the line in his other hand as it popped up near him. Now stretched between the two lines, Clovis used his last ounce of strength to push the two lines together.

Clovis held on tight as he felt the brakes bite against the wheels. The sound was immediate and deafening. Clovis shut his eyes and tried to concentrate on blocking out the noise. Clovis knew he must not fail. The whole train lurched hard as the wheels screeched against the pressure of the brakes. It was working; the train was slowing down.

Just as Clovis had thought, the station was packed full of wet, weary travelers waiting to go home. The people on the platform could hear the commotion before they could see the train. The storm had nearly blackened everything beyond the lights inside the station. Almost all the people covered their ears as the echo of the

24

screeching brakes reached a fever pitch inside the station. Suddenly the light on the front car broke though the darkness as the train approached. Everyone froze as time seemed to slow down with the train screaming toward the station. Clovis kept his eyes shut and held on as he felt the train come to a complete stop—just mere inches from the next train on the track. The sound of the brakes still pounded inside his head, but there was no crash. Clovis had done it—he had saved the train.

None of the people above, on the train or on the platform, had any idea that a mouse had risked his life and saved the day, but all the mice did! Those living at the station and near the tracks had seen Clovis clinging to the brake line, and word spread like wildfire throughout the community. An inquiry later would reveal how the cats failed to clear the debris, and all the mice would get their jobs back. But tonight—it was time for a party.

That night there was a huge celebration, and everyone came over to congratulate Clovis on his heroic feat. The mice family and their friends celebrated late into the night. At that moment, Clovis knew where he belonged and made his mind up to join Papa, and find adventure, as an Amsterdam Centraal safety engineer.

After the party, Mama was in the kitchen cleaning up when Grandpa and Zuri walked in. Zuri was so excited to recount Clovis's exploits you'd have thought it was Zuri who stopped the train and saved all those passengers.

"It's getting late, Zuri, and you have school tomorrow," Mama said. "Grandpa, take Zuri upstairs and put him to bed. It's way past his bedtime. I will finish up here in the kitchen."

Zuri protested, but Mama was firm. Zuri and Grandpa made their way up the stairs. "I can't wait to grow up and work on the railroad and be a hero, just like Clovis!" Zuri said with excitement and a little bit of a yawn.

"Yes, yes," Grandpa replied to Zuri. "It sure has been an exciting day."

Tucking Zuri in, Grandpa leaned over to kiss him goodnight. "But—" Grandpa began with a wink, "did I ever tell you about the time I lost my tail?"

THE END

About the Author

Mark Kash is a retired US Air Force veteran, a world traveler, an avid photographer, and loves classic rock and foldable maps. He was born in Newton, Kansas, and graduated from the University of La Verne in California. His favorite writer is Douglas Adams, author of *The Hitchhiker's Guide to the Galaxy*. One of his favorite quotes is from his high school English teacher, Mr. Brown, who once told him, "The sign of a budding writer is one who writes on napkins."

Mark has often said his favorite thing is an open road and a full tank of gas and has traveled the United States coast to coast multiple times. He lived in Germany for seven years and has traveled to nearly every country in Europe. But one of his favorites was the Netherlands, where he observed a mouse on the tracks of the Amsterdam Centraal Station that soon became the inspiration for this book. When not traveling, you can find Mark enjoying board games, card games, taking photos—and folding maps.

CPSIA information can be obtained
at www.ICGtesting.com
Printed in the USA
LVHW020111231021
701263LV00003B/6